Every new generation of children is enthralled by the famous stories in our Well-loved Tales series. Younger ones love to have the story read to them. Older children will enjoy the exciting stories in an easy-to-read text.

Published by Ladybird Books Ltd Loughborough Leicestershire UK
Ladybird Books Inc Lewiston Maine 04240 USA

The Town Mouse and the Country Mouse

retold for easy reading
by ANNE McKIE

illustrated by KEN McKIE

Ladybird Books

Down a country lane, deep in the roots of an old tree, lived Country Mouse. He was busy all day long finding food for the winter.

Late one night, Country Mouse
was very surprised to see his cousin
Town Mouse, coming down the
lane to visit him.

"Look out!" shouted Country Mouse, as he saw an Owl swooping down to grab Town Mouse. He gave him a big push into the ditch, and the Owl flew away. What a fright they both had.

"Welcome to my home," said Country Mouse. "You will love the country. It's so nice and quiet. I hope you can stay for a long time."

Country Mouse made a big supper.
But Town Mouse did not like the
plain food, or the thick mugs and
plates.

At bedtime Town Mouse did not like his little straw bed. It made him scratch and sneeze.

"It's too dark, and too quiet in the country," said Town Mouse.

"I can't sleep."

So Country Mouse gave him more candles and a hot drink.

Every morning before the sun was
up Country Mouse was busy
finding food for the winter.
"Come and help me, cousin,"

said Country Mouse.

Town Mouse did not like to help.

He did not like to work, and he

did not like to get his clothes and

hands dirty.

One day when they were sitting in
a cornfield, a hawk grabbed Town
Mouse, and flew away with him.
"Oh no!" cried Country Mouse.
"That is the end of poor Town
Mouse."

But the smoke from Town Mouse's
cigar made the hawk sniff and
sneeze, and he dropped Town
Mouse into a haystack.

One morning they crossed the
meadow to find mushrooms.
"I don't like the country,"
sighed Town Mouse. "It's dark,
it's cold, it's wet,
and too QUIET."

The horse who lived in the meadow
came to make friends with the
mice. Town Mouse was so
surprised he fell head over heels
into the wet grass.

"Oh, cousin," said Town Mouse, "I am tired of the country. In the town it is warm and dry, and there is no need to look for food. You must come and see for yourself."

Late one night, Town Mouse saw the family at the end of the lane getting into the car to go to town. "Come on, Country Mouse," he yelled. "Let's go."

They hid in the car, and jumped
out in the middle of town. Country
Mouse had never heard such an

awful noise, or seen so many

lights.

"This is where I live," said Town Mouse. How big the house was. How happy his family were to see Town Mouse with his country cousin.

What a welcome the town mice
gave Country Mouse. What lovely
food, fruit, cakes, biscuits, cream

and chocolate.

It was all too rich and sweet for

Country Mouse.

Town Mouse and his family took
Country Mouse round the house. It
was all too BIG for poor Country
Mouse.

At bedtime Country Mouse did not like his little soft bed. The room was too bright from the lights in the street.

Next day they went for a picnic in the park. But the pelicans and the ducks ate their food and made them run away.

A dog chased Country Mouse
under a litter basket, but Town
Mouse sprayed the dog with
lemonade. What a fright they both
had.

Back at the house, Country Mouse
was almost sucked into the carpet
cleaner. How unhappy he was.

The very next day he was saved
from a trap by Town Mouse and
his family. But they were all seen
by the CAT. They ran for their
lives back to a hole in the wall.

The CAT stayed in the room all day and all night. The mice were very hungry. They had no food at all.

That night Country Mouse had a dream of home. He smelled the trees and the earth. How he wished he was back at home.

In the morning the smell of trees was real. It was Christmas and someone had put a tree in the room. Under the tree was a hamper. "It's going near your home," cried Town Mouse.

Country Mouse could go home. He jumped into the hamper just as it was being put into the van.

Country Mouse tumbled out of the
van, into the lane where he lived.
He could hear church bells.
It was Christmas Eve.

Country Mouse ran to the church.
He knew that all the other country
mice would be there to sing
Christmas carols.

"Come, Country Mouse," said the littlest mouse. "You can spend all Christmas telling us all your great

adventures."

Country Mouse breathed a long sigh.

All he wanted to do was FORGET!